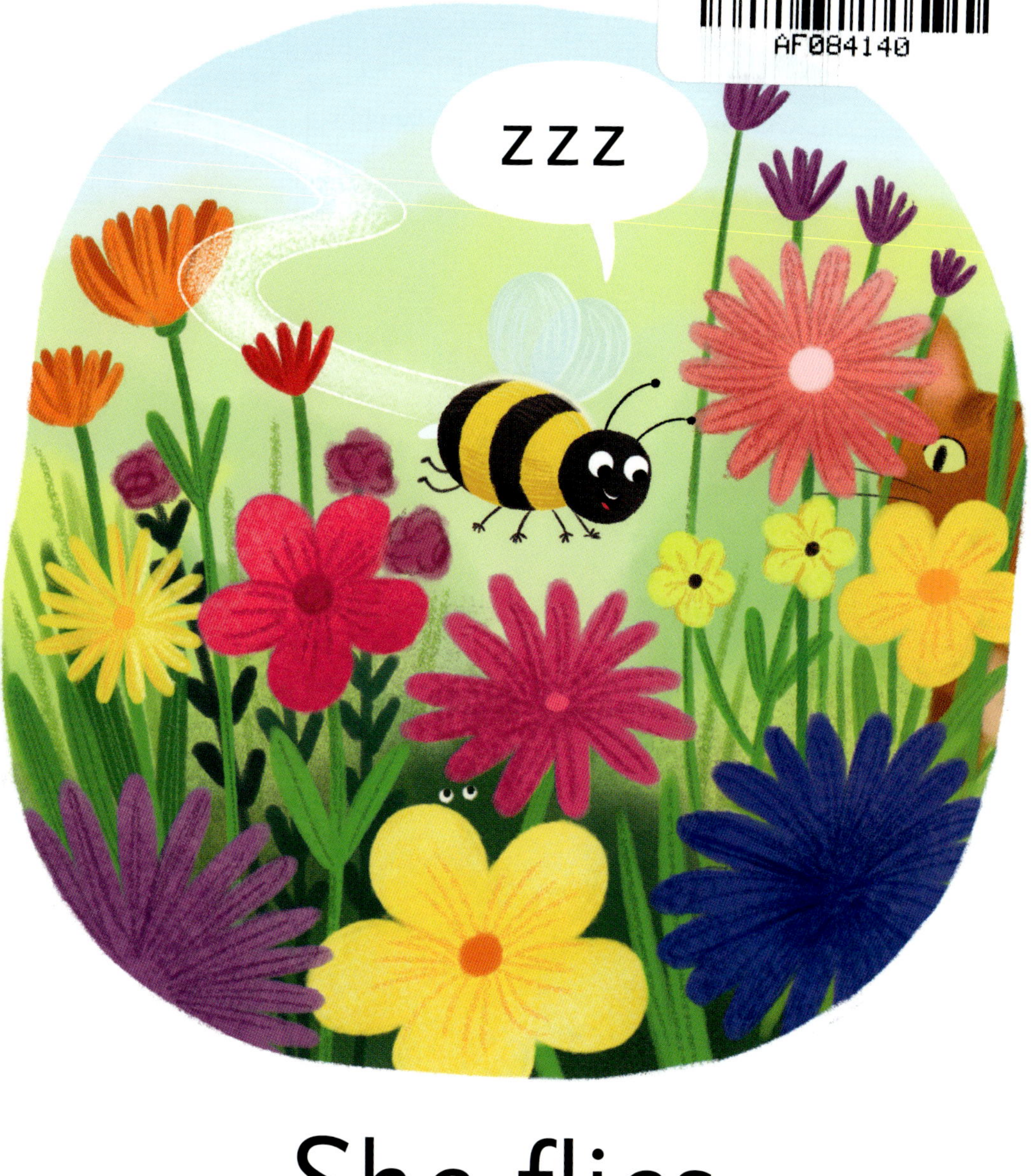

She flies.

He slithers along.

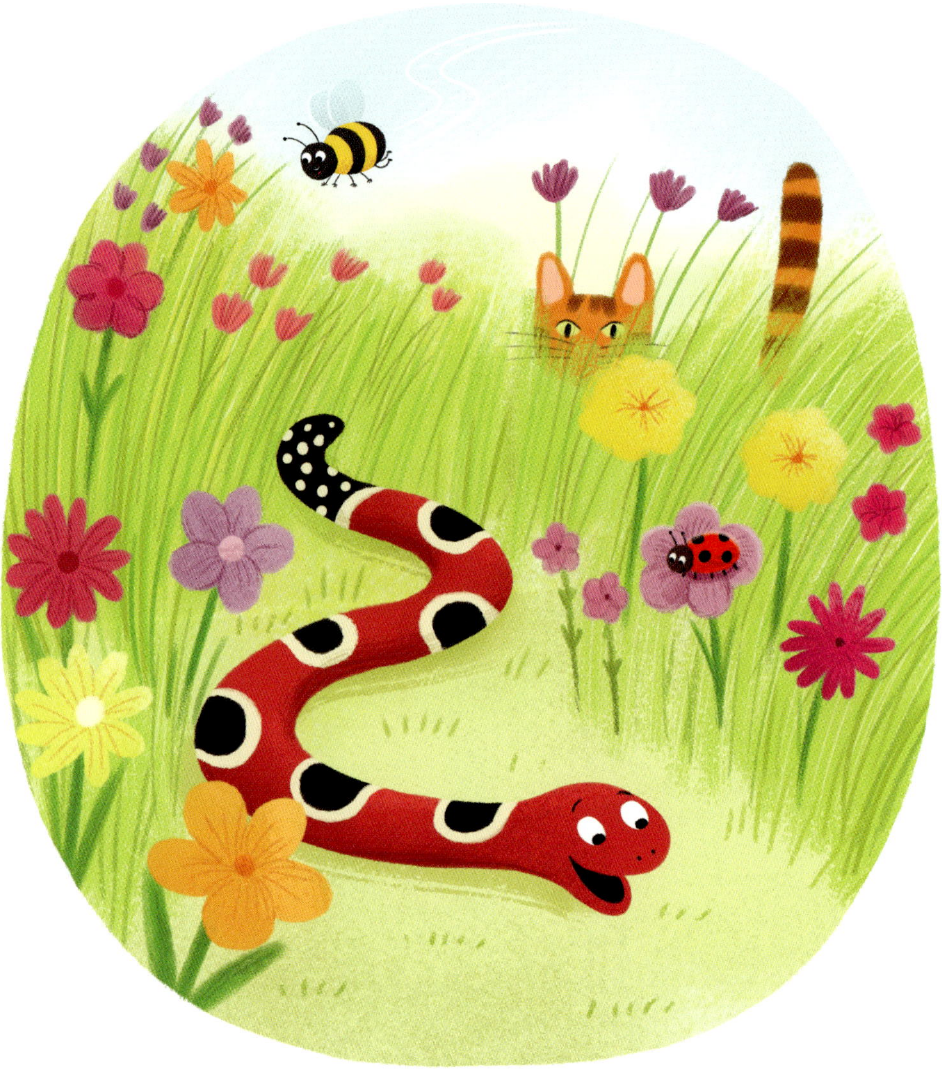

She hops,

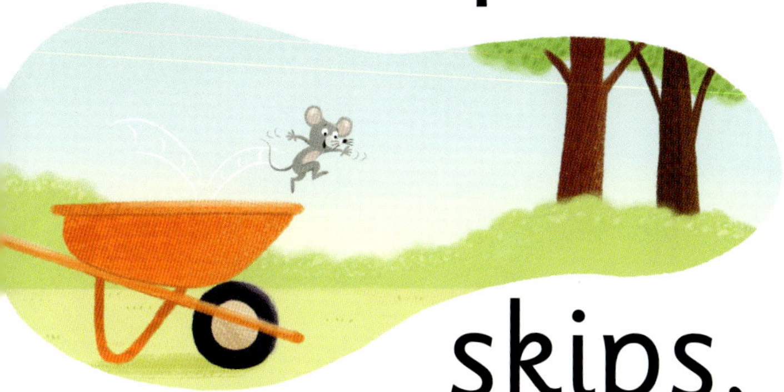

skips,

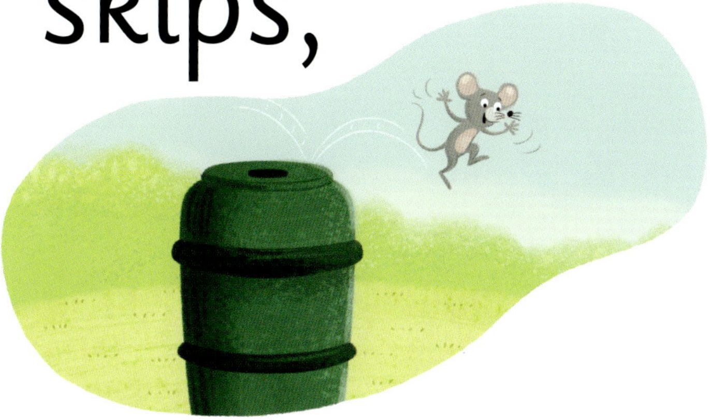

jumps!

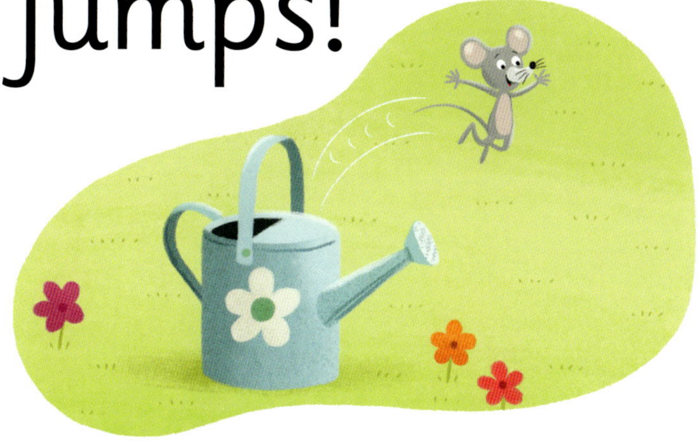

A cat!

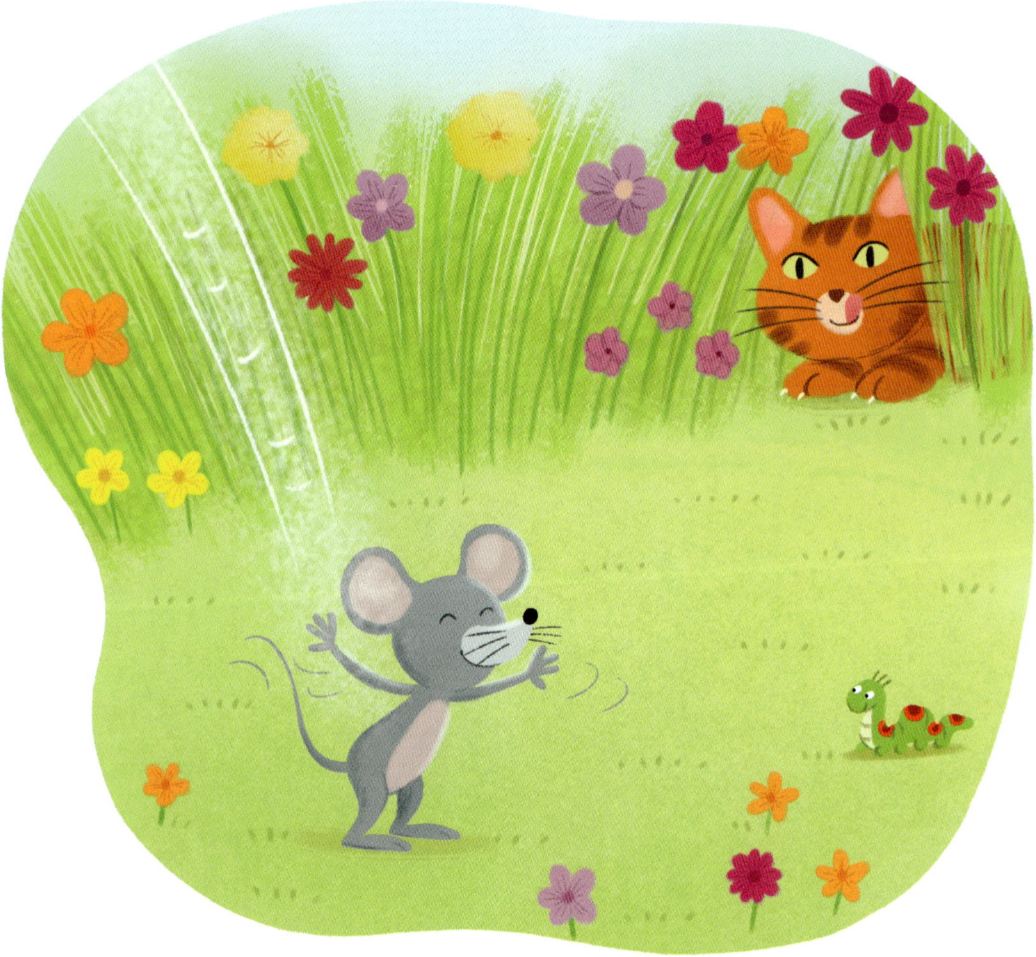

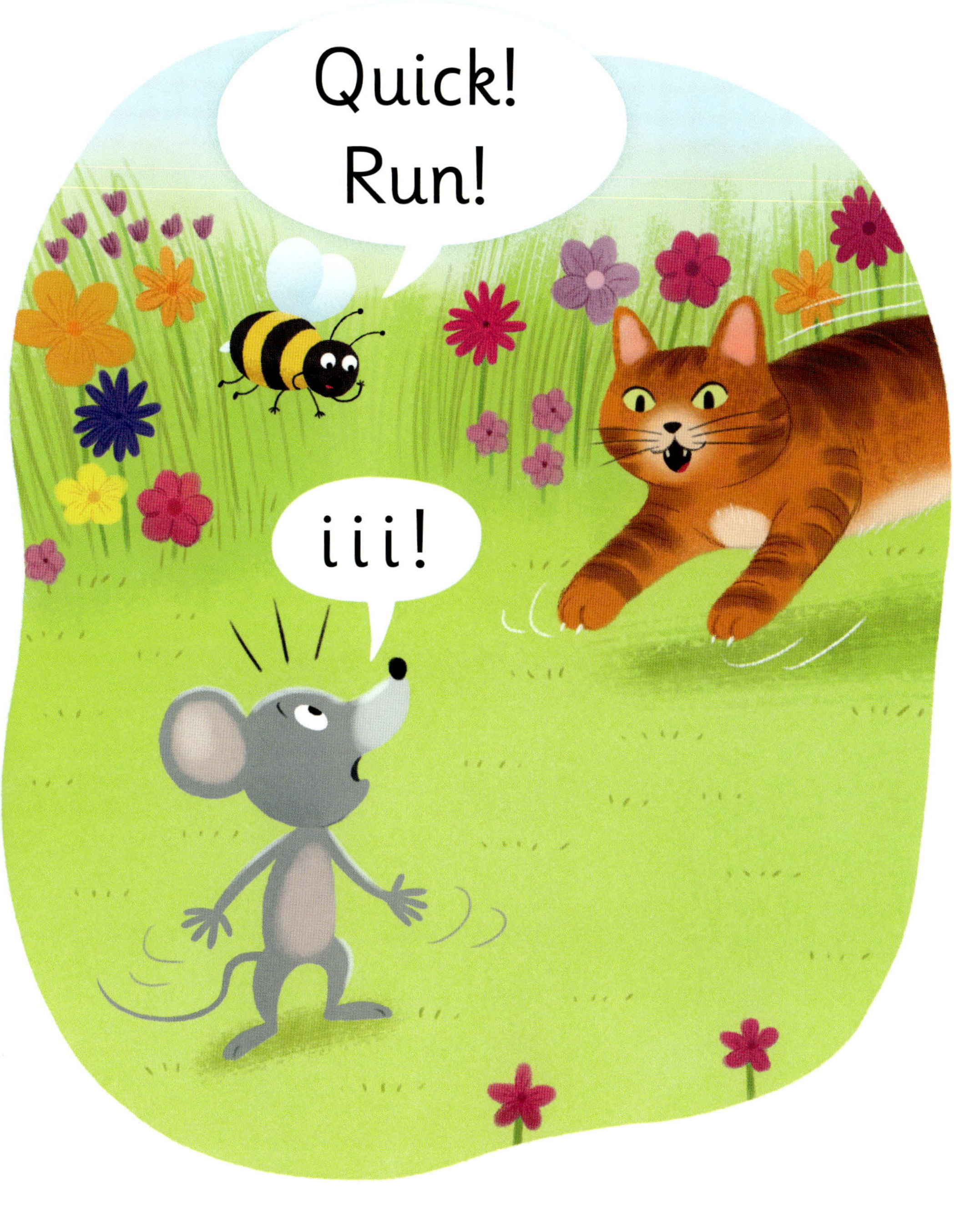
Quick! Run!
iii!

"Help!" she shouts.

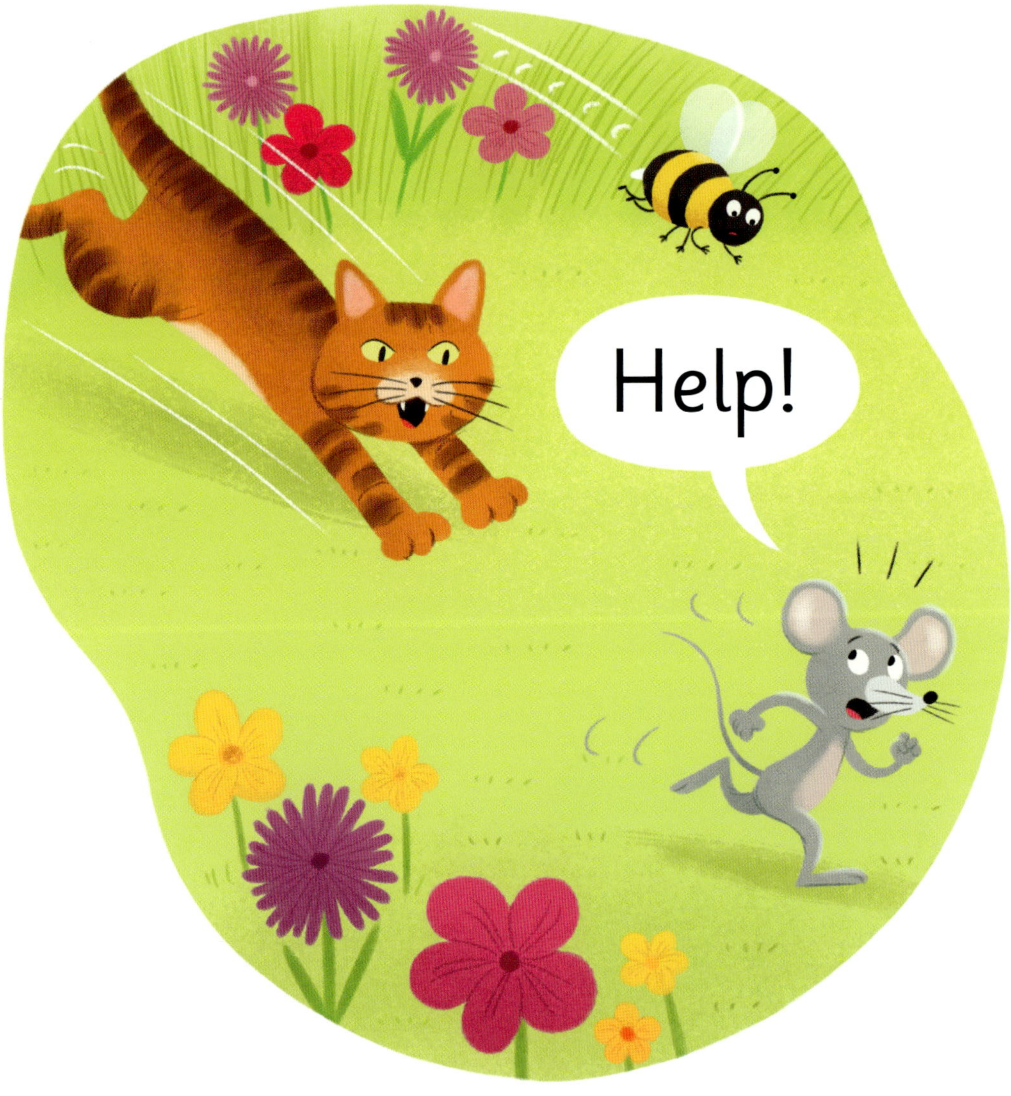

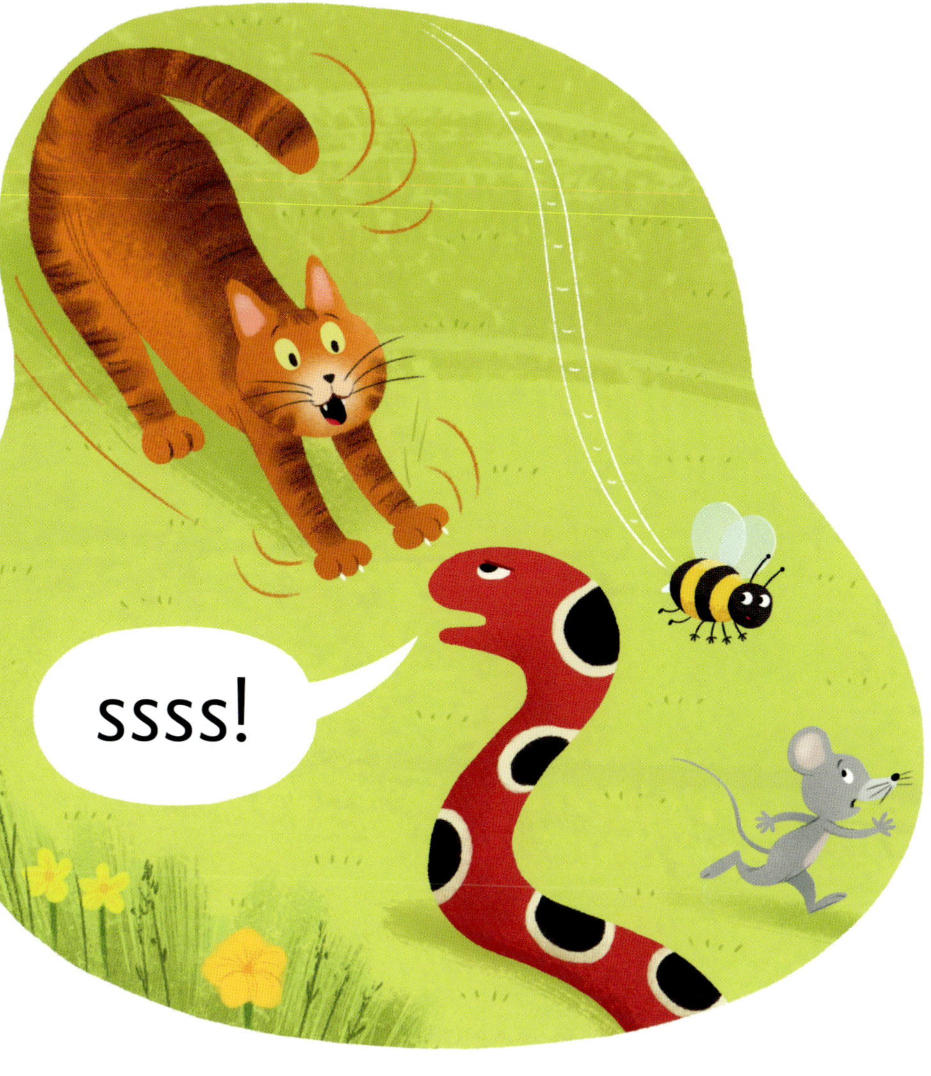

The cat stops.

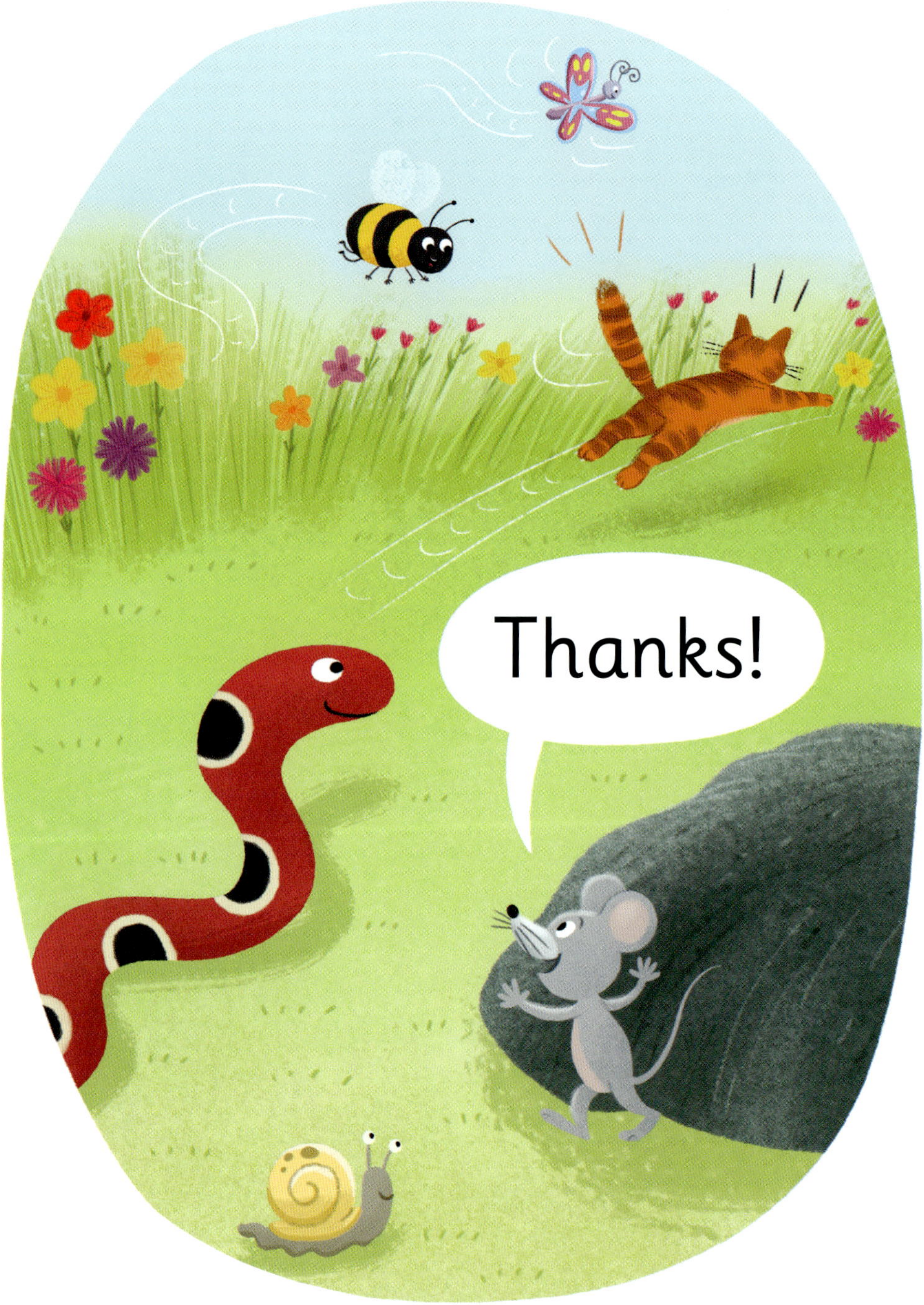
Thanks!